EDGES

Vanish

Book 8

Bjorn Esterday Was Not Born Yesterday

Wynter Sommers

GJ dePillis

Published by Pure Force Enterprises, Inc.
California, USA
Since 2002

ISBN-13: 978-1-7184-0009-2
ISBN-10: 1-7184-0009-8

DEDICATION

To all of us whose hearts reach out to change the world around, whose minds calculate the next strategic move, whose souls crave adventure and value the freedoms of democracy. To the spirit harnessing the power of fiction to alter our reality, making the world a better place for everyone.

Bjorn Series Alternate Reading Plan

1st   Edges Book 1
2nd   Edges Book 2
3rd   Gone Book 1
4th   Firebrand Book 1
5th   Edges Book 3
6th   Firebrand Book 2
7th   Gone Book 2
8th   Gone Book 3
9th   Firebrand Book 3
10th   Gone Book 4
11th   Firebrand Book 4
12th   Gone Book 5
13th   Gone Book 6
14th   Edges Book 4
15th   Firebrand Book 5
16th   Gone Book 7
17th   Firebrand Book 6
18th   Gone Book 8
19th   Firebrand Book 7
20th   Gone Book 9
21st   Firebrand Book 8
22nd   Gone Book 10
23rd   Gone Book 11
24th   Gone Book 12
25th   Gone Book 13
26th   Firebrand Book 9 (End)
27th   Gone Book 14
28th   Gone Book 15
29th   Gone Book 16
30th   Gone Book 17
31st   Gone Book 18 (End)
32nd   Edges Book 5
33rd   Edges Book 6
34th   Edges Book 7
35th   Edges Book 8
36th   Edges Book 9 (End)

CONTENTS

ACKNOWLEDGMENTS

To all those gentle souls who have graciously given tokens of love, hope, and kind considerations to others.

0 Preface

Alexandra uses athletics to get some answers. Will Sarah also get the answers she needs?

What will Sarah, Bjorn and Alexandra do with the new information they learn? If they turn the information over to the wrong people, all three of them risk a quick and sudden death.   Can they protect themselves?

Can   Sarah   believe   Alexandra's explanation, or   is   it   another   lie   to confuse Sarah?

What is the implication of the device that Alexandra demonstrates to Sarah and Bjorn?

Is the issue really about toxic dumping? Or is it, in fact, about who has the right to rule the Courtly kingdom?

1 CHAPTER Year 2036: I Looked The Other Way (Continuous Ch 75)

It was late, but Sammy Scribe, editor of The Daily Memo, was still in his office, locked in a heated discussion with Bjorn. Outside Sammy's office, the cleaning crew were busy sweeping up and emptying trashcans.

"Look," Sammy warned, barely holding back his anger, "As the Editor of the Daily Memo, I need verifiable proof!" He shrugged, "OK! I know top brass forced me to force you, Bjorn, to get out of investigative reporting into what should be called 'Lifestyle celebrity gossip'. I get that you don't think your skills are being used. I get that politics made me cave in from the goal of true freedom of the press. But remember...."

"Sammy," Bjorn interrupted, "You offered me Sarah Paradise's contact info in exchange for covering a simple Conference Center speaker story. I had no idea that it would yank my life away for five years, but I got you an incredible journal series out of it... Please, Sammy... you just have to trust me. I cannot reveal my sources..."

Sammy shook his head, "Got it. I remember. Yeah, you vanished for five years, but at the end you gave me a feature that sold so many paper copies, I was able to push back on laying off other reporters and reject having robots do the writing. Yeah, your final exposé from when you were gone saved jobs, saved the paper version of our beloved Daily Memo. Your story kept us all going... That's why I never questioned you about the time you were gone, Bjorn... But now you have rejoined us as an employee of the Daily Memo." Sammy lowered his voice. "Skipper Courtly has got spies everywhere... Please! See things from the viewpoint of the editor's desk trying to keep a paper running... I cannot just go on your instinct, your scraps of what you call 'evidence'. I need genuine proof!"

"I've got more than just pieces of evidence," Bjorn retorted, "...I almost have the edges of the whole puzzle put together, Sammy. You've got to trust my hunch."

"I can't afford hunches, anymore." Almost angry, Sammy shook his head. "The public doesn't want facts and truth like they did twenty years ago. They only want fashion and fluff to distract them from their miserable lives."

"Sammy, it'll be big. Real big," Bjorn tried to persuade.

"You have a chat with a little Earthie girl and now you want me to cash in a favor? I just don't..." Sammy's voice trailed off.

Bjorn pointed to the communication device in Sammy's ear. "You got to make the call."

Sammy folded his arms and pressed back in his chair, thinking.

Bjorn placed both palms on the edge of Sammy's desk, leaning across without breaking eye contact. "Sammy, I'm telling you, he won't be taking any transportation that can be traced."

Bjorn abruptly turned away and walked to a stack of newspapers Sammy had piled up on his table, and pulled one out from the middle of the stack.

"Hey, those are this month's copies! Don't mess up the order on those. They go to Library archives next week," Sammy protested.

Bjorn turned open a page, folded it back, then slapped it down on Sammy's desk.

With calm measured control, Bjorn said to Sammy, "I know where he'll be and when he will be there. I'm handing it to you - a plan on how to get him. But, we have to act now. Come on, Sammy. Your call. I know it's a hunch. But trust me." Bjorn paused. "What's it gonna be?"

2 CHAPTER Year 2036: Celery (Continuous Ch 76)

Outside Sarah's place, young Joshua waited in a horse and buggy, ready to take Alexandra back home. Sarah peered out her window.

"He's here. Obviously your village got the message I left at the Inn when we cancelled your reservation," Sarah smiled at Alexandra.

On the table were remnants of the baked cloud they had for breakfast. Two bowls stained with chocolate ice cream from the night before sat in Sarah's kitchen sink, waiting to be washed.

6

"He has been a good brother to me, Miss Paradise. I was going to take the bus back, but it looks as if he'd rather escort me home."

Sarah smiled, "I think he took the job at the corporation to keep an eye on you, Alexandra. To keep you safe."

Alexandra replied, "Papa Lantz did release him from his duties to come into the city and work with me. I couldn't have done any of this without his support."

Alexandra crossed to the door. Sarah walked with her.

"I apologize for repeating the obvious, but you do realize," Sarah stated, concerned, "that Noah Lantz is not your real father and Joshua is not your blood brother."

"Of course I do, Miss Paradise," Alexandra replied with a grin. "By the way, I appreciate you not telling Pip or any of the Courtly execs that I was the source of the information in that file. I thank God Mr. Esterday got you out of the castle before..." Her voice trailed off.

"Yes. Sometimes I wonder what made him return to the castle that night," Sarah commented.

"Oh, he told me," Alexandra explained. "It was because the lady at the florist was explaining how to calculate volume for a small pond. Then, he remembered the boat in the Castle lake. He figured out that the tides of that lake come in every other day. Out there, rare biurnal tides rush in fast and pull out faster than a regular tide. So, every other day, lake water would seep into the basement, flooding it up to the ceiling making it appear that the coffin was emanating powers to toss the statues around."

"I saw that coffin when I was down there," Sarah interjected. "I'll bet that ornate iron work at the base weighed it down so that it was the only object that didn't float around."

Alexandra nodded, "No ghost. Just physics. God even used mundane circumstances to bring Bjorn to you in time, Miss Paradise."

Alexandra picked up her quilting bag.

"I should go to Joshua, now. Be safe, Miss Paradise."

Sarah opened the door, then gave Alexandra a big hug goodbye.

"Yes, Alexandra. Be safe."

Sarah closed the door behind her.

Alexandra put her quilting bag in the buggy, but wanted to ride up next to Joshua on the way home.

"I missed you, Joshua."

He smiled at her. "Has staying the night in the city made you forget the beauty of our countryside?" he asked, as their horse clip-clopped along the side of the road. Vehicles whizzed past them.

"The country nights are much more peaceful than the evening I just had in that city," Alexandra said.

Then there was silence as they continued to travel. Gradually, the traffic faded and they became the only ones on the now narrow country road.

"Have you noticed," Joshua stated, "that Papa has planted extra celery this season."

"Oh?" She asked, "I love it when Mama Lantz makes her celery stuffing for a grand feast, but it usually takes three weeks to get everything ready. Is somebody in the village getting married or something?"

"I'm... I'm not sure... uh... Lexi... Working with you as an intern... um... Lexi... has made me appreciate the unusual gifts God has given you, unlike the other girls in the village," Joshua stammered.

"Oh, Joshua. You know the elders tried everything to get the company to stop that polluting of our fields. I just figured if I got a job at the headquarters, I might have a chance to make a difference and get the dumping halted," Alexandra replied.

"I was worried about you, Lexi." He glanced at her quickly and bit his lip.

"You know I'd do anything to make sure you were safe, Alexandra Lantz. Anything."

She smiled at him, "I know, Joshua. I'm blessed to have made the acquaintance of a man like you."

He smiled back, "I am so sorry your parents died and you had to live a life devoid of finery, knowing your own real father could never give you away at a wedding... but I think you thrive in our village... or would you prefer to leave our home and work at Courtly full-time?"

"No, Joshua. I like living with your parents... my dear adopted parents... our village." Alexandra smiled reassuringly and put her head on his shoulder as he held the reins.

"I have not yet been baptized in the faith," Joshua bashfully blurted. "I can choose... to marry... outside. I mean, not outdoors... an outsider... and still use the celery Papa planted... for a meal... a feast... wedding feast... If that person would agree to be my... would you... wife... that is?"

Joshua gave her a shy glance. He could not tell if her expression was one of happy surprise or utter dismay...

3 CHAPTER Year 2036: Inside the Violin (Continuous Ch 77)

Sarah washed the dishes in her sink, then looked out the window. She didn't have a job to rush to, so she had a free, quiet afternoon. Perhaps she'd go window shopping on such a lovely day.

Downtown was bustling with activity. It was nice being around people, she thought. She must get Bjorn something for being such an angel. It was still astonishing to realize he had saved her life! As she passed by one

13

store window, she saw a tiny harp shaped paperweight.

"Perfect. Bjorn was my guardian angel and angels play harps!" she thought to herself as she walked in.

Clerk Joe was talking to Clerk John. The music store was crowded as usual and the two clerks were involved in discussing some account on their computer screen.

Customers milled about. Sarah started to ask a question, but she didn't want to interrupt the clerk's conversation. She stood, waiting, busying herself with examining the display.

"Did you send him a bill or did he pay credits in the store?" Clerk John asked Clerk Joe.

"The other guy paid, but it was that Earthie boy who picked up Mr. Courtly's violin," Clerk Joe replied.

"It couldn't have been an Earthie. They don't work for large corporations and especially not as an errand boy for an executive! Look, just close the record putting in the name of the guy who paid. Forget about that Earthie kid. You don't remember his name, anyway."

Sarah listened for a moment, then immediately left the shop uncertain how to interpret what she'd just overheard. Was it possible the Earth Farmer boy they mentioned was Joshua Lantz? Would Joshua have a motive to harm Skipper Courtly? How could Joshua ever have used a violin to kill the dead C.E.O.?

She tapped her ear to initialize her

com device. Bjorn did not answer. She walked up and down the block a few times trying to think.

Then, she walked back into the crowded music store. Opera was playing in the background... some famous soprano.

"Excuse me. Could you show me that tiny harp in the window?" Sarah asked Clerk John.

When Clerk John returned with the paperweight, Sarah asked, "If I were to get something repaired here, how would it be delivered to me?"

The clerk answered her. Sarah thanked him, as he gift wrapped the little harp. Holding the colorful bag, she left the music store.

She tried calling Bjorn, again. Still no

answer.

She hesitated a moment, then marched straight to the nearest Soldier Police headquarters.

The drone at the front desk voice-printed Sarah and took her picture, then admitted her inside where she found a human.

"Yes. May I speak to whoever is reviewing the death of Mr. Skipper Courtly?"

After some time a man approached her.

"Teacher Paradise?" The SP asked. Sarah nodded. He continued, "Detective Gene is not available right now. Are you contributing information about the Courtly case or...?"

Sarah and he spoke, but he was not forthcoming with any real information. He simply repeated, "Teacher Paradise, I understand your point, but didn't you read the Daily Memo newspaper yesterday? All the information is covered in there. I can't give you any more details of the case than has already been put in the public record."

"Well," Sarah shrugged her shoulders, "I missed that issue. Would it be possible for you to just tell me... as long as I'm here?"

The SP walked to a table at the side of the room and picked up the Daily Memo newspaper from yesterday, handing it to Sarah.

"Read it for yourself. Remnants of a thin glass vial," the SP started, "appear to have been mounted inside the body of the violin. When it shattered, it released a localized gas which we cannot identify. This gas, it seems, killed Mr. Courtly on the stage, but those in the audience were not affected."

"Gas?"

"If you have information about this case, I can take your statement," he offered.

Then, he indicated the Daily Memo newspaper in Sarah's hands. "Did you know the deceased?"

"I used to work for his son," she answered scanning the paper he had just handed to her. "What would make it shatter? The vial, I mean?" Sarah asked, curious.

"Fine lead crystal like that?" the SP started, "We've been told it would have to be something as loud as a jackhammer. Conversation is usually measured at about 50 decibels, so they are telling us it'd have to be about twice that to shatter the glass. But it's just a theory that sound waves resonate with glass in that way. Just a theory."

"Any fingerprints? DNA? Aura prints?" Sarah pleaded, "Anything else?"

"How about if we ask the questions, now, Teacher Paradise? Please have a seat."

4 CHAPTER Year 2036: Changing Pictures (Continuous Ch 78)

What Sarah Paradise thought would be a five minute chat at the SP headquarters turned into two hours of a formal interrogation. Definitely not the way she had planned to spend her free afternoon.

Stressed and exhausted, Teacher Paradise hoped her comments had not been twisted or misinterpreted. Sarah supposed she could have walked out at any time, but felt intimidated by the cameras, security-bots, and official uniforms. For a moment, she even thought she might be arrested, but at

21

last they had simply thanked her for her voluntary statement and let her go.

To recuperate from the ordeal, she decided to make her way to Library.

The SP had mentioned some things that made her curious to do a bit of fact-checking. She found her favorite seat near a window, sat in silence for a moment, then spent some time studying.

Finally, she gathered up her notes and made her way quietly to the always pleasant Mrs. Libris to whisper a grateful thanks.

Sarah caught a bus and went across town to the office of The Daily Memo. She searched for Editor Sammy Scribe's name on the directory before making her way to the right floor.

The newspaper office was a bustling hum of noise with employees walking very quickly from one end to the other. They all seemed to be in a rush.

She saw Sammy heading toward the break room.

"Mr. Scribe!" she called across the room, but it was so noisy, he didn't hear at first. She called again, louder this time.

Sammy Scribe turned around. She hurried to him.

"I'm looking for Bjorn, Mr. Scribe. He's not answering my calls. Could you please tell me where you've sent him?"

"I haven't sent him anywhere. Maybe he's taking the day off."

"No. I've been to his place. He's not there. He didn't leave me a note, and he's not answering his com. I need to find him," Sarah persisted.

Sammy looked at his empty mug, then at Sarah. "Why don't you wait for me in my office over there," he pointed across the room. "I'll be just a minute."

He walked off.

Sarah headed toward his office.

Once inside, she looked around at the chaos of a creative mind pressed by too many deadlines. Awards were pushed back against the top of a bookshelf. Older electronic pictures covered the walls with ever changing images of Sammy with important people. The photographs dissolved from picture to picture every few seconds. It made her dizzy to be in a room where all the photo images kept shifting.

Sammy Scribe's office was cluttered with these photographs.

Soon, he returned, happy with his cup full. He was surprised to see her.

"What, you're still here?"

Sarah replied, "You just asked me to wait in your office, Mr. Scribe."

"I was being polite," he said. "I was hoping you'd get bored and leave." He slumped down into his chair, looking at the piles of work in front of him on his messy desk. "Look. I'm busy. Make it snappy."

"I just want to know where Bjorn is," she said

"Who?" he shrugged.

"Bjorn Esterday. Investig... Lifestyles division," she corrected herself.

"Now, why did you want to see Bjorn?" Sammy started as he added a dash of spirits to his coffee, then sipped it, contented.

"I was at Library and happened across a redmail in a huge collection of archived Courtly redmails."

"And why are old redmails so important?" Sammy asked indicating boredom by drumming his fingers on the desk. "I really have a lot of work to do, here. Some of us have jobs."

"This particular redmail I found appears to have been received by the Courtly offices. It announced Jack Courtly's death."

"That's old news. Seven years old! I know Bjorn wouldn't care about that because I don't care about that!" Sammy laughed.

Sarah got up and paced. Then she

decided to just tell Sammy her concern. She produced a small electronic note tablet.

"You see, Mr. Scribe," Sarah explained, "It doesn't just say Jack Courtly is presumed dead in the train wreck. It's from an unusual redmail account- somebody named Percy Snatcher- asking for payment for Jack Courtly's death. Is it possible Jack Courtly was murdered? I found another redmail from Skipper Courtly on that same day, sent to another corporate city, agreeing to sell that other corporation bio weapons to fortify their SP forces, which would deplete our own Courtly SP armory."

"What are you saying?" Sammy muttered, jaw clenched.

"I'm guessing Skipper Courtly wanted to supplement his income by selling these weapons to help competing corporations expand their territories. Maybe to secretly fund the AnCors. Either way, Skipper acted against Courtly Corp interests." She watched him. "Won't Bjorn want to see these?"

"So, you're accusing a recently departed executive of breaking Earth Farmer anti-dumping agreements, shortcutting to profit unethically, and not caring who it damaged?" Sammy bluntly demanded.

"Well, it appears, by these Redmails, that he was willing to even sell out this company, Mr. Scribe. His own corporation! They must have offered him a lot of money to make that worthwhile. And if he wasn't getting money from legit business profits as well as Jack Courtly's estate..." She shrugged.

As she waited for his response, her eye caught a photograph changing on the wall behind him. It became an image of Pip Courtly, with Skipper shaking hands with... Sammy Scribe. Then, another one of the same three fishing together. Then, yet another of the three of them at a formal dinner. Skipper was holding his violin.

"Mr. Scribe," Sarah started cautiously. "Which 'top brass' asked for the reorg closing down the Daily Memo's

Investigative Reporting division? Nearly making Bjorn lose his job?"

"Why don't you have a seat, Miss Paradise," Sammy said. "Stay a while."

5 CHAPTER- Year 2036: Faded And Disappeared (Continuous Ch 79)

Bjorn Esterday left the lab with results in hand. Finally, some progress.

He secured a rental vehicle, since a local body shop was repairing his. The damage resulting from that night he was pursued by two self-driving vehicles turned out to be much more extensive than he had thought. The mechanics at first warned him that he would probably never be able to drive it again, but Bjorn was hopeful repairs could be made.

He drove his rental to a large imposing unmarked building just outside of town and sat, waiting.

His com device didn't seem to get

reception in this area.

Eventually, at the far end of the building, he spied a lumbering truck emerge from a warehouse door. Its gears cranked as it eased onto the road, obviously laden down by a heavy cargo.

In his newly rented vehicle, Bjorn followed the truck as it headed along an empty road to the countryside on this sunny afternoon.

He wished he could stop what was about to happen, but he had to be an impartial observer, capturing just the unbiased facts. He turned on a dashboard video camera and zoomed in on the truck now a good distance in front of him. Only an occasional car passed him on the almost empty road.

The rear of the truck displayed a cartoon depicting a happy bear and deer on it with the words "Mayfounder. We do it right."

He needed to see where it went.

There was a fork in the road. Maybe he

was getting too close. The road branching to the left went down to the farm lands. The road to the right went uphill into the forest.

The truck stopped at the fork, not indicating which road it would take. Bjorn knew he couldn't stop as well, since it would look suspicious. Assuming this driver would take the left road, Bjorn sped up, driving around the truck taking the right fork uphill.

The area was forested. Finally, out of sight of the truck, he found a narrow path. Bjorn drove his rental in among thick shadowy trees, concealing the vehicle from the road. He parked and got out, grabbing a pair of binoculars and his camera.

Bjorn knew that today no one would be working in the Earth Farmer fields, since it was their day of worship. Perfect for clandestine dumping.

Bjorn found a spot, which kept him concealed, yet gave him a clear line of sight to the freshly plowed farmland below. With camera now focused on the truck, Bjorn waited.

The truck was moving again.

"I knew you'd take the left fork. I knew it!" Bjorn smiled to himself.

He started his camera.

After a few moments, the truck stopped and the driver got out, dressed in protective clothing that may have been better suited for space walks than simply dumping supposedly "safe" waste-material. The driver opened a valve on the truck releasing a liquid that, at first, colored the farm land a bright florescent green which rapidly faded, and then disappeared, as it was absorbed into the soil. A clearly visible gas emanated from the surface, then dissipated into the air.

Bjorn recorded the dumping, and the man quickly got back into his truck and nervously drove off.

Bjorn filmed that truck driving back up the road. Then, he saw a deer on the plowed field and focused the camera on this sublime creature. It stepped across the freshly plowed field where the substance had just been dumped.

The deer suddenly wobbled and shivered violently, just as witnesses described Skipper Courtly after he played his violin. The deer collapsed and then lay motionless.

A moment later, a rabbit came hopping by, paused at the body of the deer, then, apparently unaffected, scampered away.

Bjorn concluded that whatever fumes killed the deer had quickly vaporized so that the rabbit did not immediately show any signs of damage. Were there long term effects? This seemed to explain why only Skipper Courtly had died and none of the audience were directly adversely impacted by the gas.

Clearly, Bjorn had just discovered what killed Skipper Courtly. He didn't know how the man had been exposed, but he had a very good idea as to who had made it happen.

He hurried back to his vehicle, and headed to town, pleased that he had just recorded proof of the dumping and deadly impacts on local wildlife.

Bjorn had to pass through one of those smaller towns that had only one stoplight.

He stopped, idling.

While he waited, he called the lab, again. Yes, they finally got a fix on the phony SP. Ten minutes ago, the fake SP, who had ransacked Sarah's place, spent credits downtown. They agreed to send a photo of the guy to Bjorn ASAP.

Now, Bjorn knew he had to get downtown fast. Impatient, he saw that the traffic light stayed on red. Red like a warning light. Blood red.

Slowly, creeping up behind him, rolled another vehicle. Bjorn noticed it in his rear view reflector.

Casually, he glanced back over his shoulder to confirm that there was... no driver. It was another one of those remote controlled jobs. There seemed to be a lot more self-driving vehicles in operation than he had ever noticed before.

Suddenly nervous, Bjorn glanced around and tried to decide what to do next.

Then, the light turned green.

6 CHAPTER Year 2036: Bjorn Calls the Foreman (Continuous Ch 80)

Bjorn drove very cautiously, obeying every traffic light. He carefully changed lanes, hoping the robotic vehicle would not recognize Bjorn's rental car and instead just go about its business.

Bjorn made a com call.

"This is Bjorn Esterday. Remember me?"

"Sure," the foreman answered on the other end. "How could I forget that flooded basement in the castle?"

"I've got to ask you. When you came down to have Skipper Courtly sign that document, you said you were looking for…but you never finished your sentence. Who or what were you looking for?"

"I wanted to see if Miss Paradise had left, yet. Oh, hey I forgot about looking for her because then Skipper Courtly went missing. But, before you arrived, I went downstairs to look for Skippie, rest his soul, and instead, guess who was in the basement?"

The foreman continued explaining to Bjorn.

Bjorn kept driving.

The remote control vehicle was still one car-length behind him.

7 CHAPTER Year 2036: Coffee with An SP (Continuous Ch 81)

Bjorn headed toward a crowded downtown area and parked. Anxiously, he looked behind him. The robotic vehicle had vanished.

His com device flashed. He had a message.

It was a photograph sent from the lab. The identity of the man, the one who pretended to be an SP at Sarah's place, was being sent to Bjorn.

Then he spotted that same man, that same fake SP, right there on the

38

sidewalk a few feet away, calmly walking into a hydration station, as if he'd done nothing. Bjorn glanced at the photo he just received. Yup. It was definitely the same guy.

Bjorn got out of his vehicle.

On a hunch, Bjorn headed down the street to the hydration station.

He passed a genuine SP and said, "Hello, Officer. How are you?"

"Greetings, Reporter Bjorn Esterday," came the reply as the SP kept walking.

Curious, Bjorn stopped and turned around, "How did you know my name without my HIB?"

The officer paused, looked at Bjorn, then replied, "Beta testing. Some units have been selected to experiment with more modern technology. Facial recognition," he smiled and went on his way.

Bjorn stopped him, again, "Officer!"

The SP turned around.

"Would I be able to buy you a cup of coffee? I just want to say thank you for all you do to keep our streets safe," Bjorn smiled.

The SP checked the time on his visor display, then agreed to accept Bjorn's offer of fine gourmet coffee.

They both walked into the hydration station.

Bjorn mentioned that he had a friend who was recently visited by a false SP. He added that the man's rude behavior showed that he could never meet the exacting standards required to become a Courtly SP. Bjorn elaborated further, that not only was the fake SP rude, but his uniform was a cheap imitation of the genuine SP regimentals.

The SP appeared sympathetic. "Some other corp-cities make cheaper gear. Some foreign places even made knock-offs of what we wear at Courtly," the SP explained as Bjorn placed their order at the counter. "The Courtly SP uniforms are better designed than the uniforms worn by other corporation SPs."

The SP leaned against the wood paneled wall as Bjorn paid the cashier for their drinks.

The SP's jacket started to morph to the exact striations in the wood, making his jacket also appear to blend into the wall.

Bjorn was keen on learning more.

"I'll wait for the coffees, if you wouldn't mind grabbing a table," Bjorn suggested as he scanned the crowded room.

He spotted the fake SP sipping coffee, reading.

"Officer, there is plenty of room over there with that guy reading the newspaper."

The SP strode authoritatively over to the man, who, when seeing he was confronted by an SP, became suddenly very nervous.

"Actor Harry Liteman..." The SP said in his customary greeting. The man jumped up, dropping his newspaper, spilling his coffee, and pushing patrons out of the way as he raced through the crowd to the exit.

The SP paused, as he read the file of Actor Harry Liteman, which appeared on the SP's visor screen.

Then, the SP pursued him.

Bjorn turned to the drinks server at the counter and said, "Take your time making those. I'll be right back."

Bjorn dashed out after the SP, turning on his recording unit in his pocket. He saw the athletic SP had caught up to this Harry Liteman, restraining him for questioning.

Without prompting, Harry started to babble, "Look!" He pleaded with the SP, "You can't take me into custody. I can't afford another strike on my record."

Bjorn caught up with them, and took his chances, shouting at Harry, "Why did you search Sarah Paradise's home?"

Harry stuttered, "I was hired. I was hired. I don't know that lady. I've been out of work! I never saw the guy who set it all up. All I know is he said if I searched everywhere and didn't find a copy of the papers somebody named Pip got from the lady, he'd leave her alone and finally pay me. I searched. She was clean. I got paid.

"Describe who paid you," Bjorn demanded.

"By some drone. That's it. Believe me," Harry pleaded.

"The guy who hired you- What else did he say?" Bjorn pressed on.

The SP looked at the reporter, lips twisted to the side as if wondering why Bjorn was interrogating this man, but curious to hear the answers himself, allowing it for the moment.

"Just how he tried to finish up something but kept getting interrupted," Harry stammered, "So now I had to do this searching a woman's condo thing dressed up like an SP. The guy just kept telling me that I better not mess up and be sure there was no other copies because he wasn't about to go back to making 50 credits an hour. I mean that's more than I get for a legit gig. What's he complaining about, right?"

"And? Anything else?" Bjorn demanded, adrenaline pumping.

"He said he may need me to work for him again. But, I won't. I totally won't ever work for him again. I swear it. Anyway, then I got paid off and I was done dealing with him." Harry sputtered, "I truly mean it! You gatta believe me." Harry was no longer the blustering obnoxious man who burst in on Sarah Paradise.

The Soldier Police asked with calm restraint, "You admit to impersonating a Courtly Soldier Police?"

"Yes, if I get leniency on the other stuff! Yes."

The SP cuffed Harry Liteman for impersonating an SP and possibly breaking and entering.

The waiter inside the hydration station came running out, holding two covered coffee cups in his hands, as he jogged to the trio on the sidewalk.

"Who gets the decaffeinated?" the server asked.

The SP jerked his head at Bjorn, "Him. He needs it."

8 CHAPTER Year 2036: Who Is Harry? (Continuous Ch 82)

As the SP officer's vehicle took off with prisoner Harry Liteman in the back seat, Bjorn trotted quickly to his rental vehicle, zipping off after them. He tried to com Sarah, but she wasn't picking up.

When he arrived at the SP main station, Bjorn parked a few feet from the entrance. He witnessed Harry Liteman getting dragged from the SP vehicle in restraints.

At the same time, he was surprised to

see Sarah and Sammy Scribe walking toward the Soldier Police station's main entrance.

Bjorn hopped out and ran, hoping to intercept his boss and Sarah.

Why were they there?

He was about three strides away when Sarah noticed Bjorn, halting Sammy to alert him of Bjorn's presence. Then, Bjorn saw the young Earth Farmer Joshua, being led toward the station, also in restraints.

"Wait. So, Pip didn't murder Skipper? It was Joshua Lantz?" Bjorn asked Sarah.

"I'm sure he's being framed," Sarah whispered quickly to Bjorn. "I just hope the statement I made isn't responsible for bringing him in. Alexandra is very upset."

"Didn't Alexandra go back home?" Bjorn asked

"Yes, but she called me," Sarah explained, "when I was talking with Sammy. She was upset Joshua was being arrested right there in front of the entire village! I feel responsible."

"The Earth Farmers have a com device there?" Bjorn asked.

"No," said Sarah, "Her village does not have coms. I don't know where she was calling from." Sarah continued, "I told her I would head to the station and look into it, but Sammy insisted on going with me. He says he got a story-alert sending him to the station, also."

She pulled back, as she noticed Sammy looking at her, and said "I don't know if Pip is totally innocent, but I really know Joshua has to be."

Sammy interrupted, "Maybe Earthie and Trust-fund baby were working together to knock off the old man."

Across the parkway they saw another SP vehicle arrive. The door opened and out stepped SP Detective Gene. He walked around to the passenger side, opened the door and reached in. They were surprised to see that he was helping Alexandra out of the vehicle.

"What is she doing here? Is she under arrest, too?" Bjorn asked.

As Gene and Alexandra passed them, Bjorn called, "Officer, why are Alexandra and Joshua Lantz being arrested?"

"Who are you?" Gene looked at Bjorn.

Sammy snapped impatient, "We're from the Daily Memo."

Alexandra interrupted, "Sir, Bjorn Esterday and Sarah Paradise are my friends. I called Sarah on your com, remember? She said she'd be here."

Gene responded to Bjorn with, "Are you here for a story or to give a statement?"

Sammy countered, "May we get your name?"

"I'm the investigating officer of the Skipper Courtly case," Gene replied.

Sammy asked again, "And your name is?"

Gene replied, "Detective Ivan Emilio Gene"

"I don't know how, but the violin was used in killing Skipper," Sarah whispered to Bjorn.

Gene stated, "Joshua Lantz is being held as a person of interest for the murder of Skipper Courtly. Alexandra is here to give a statement. That answers your question. Now, what information on the case can you enlighten me with?"

"I witnessed," Bjorn started, "Joshua bring in the violin case at the party, but he did not open it. Pip took the case and brought the case to the front of the stage. I don't supposed your autopsy revealed that Skipper was killed by an untraceable gaseous substance, did it?"

Surprised, Sammy turned to Bjorn, "Why do you ask that?"

"Because," Bjorn replied, "I just got on visual record some toxic dumping. A deer evidenced the same symptoms that Skipper Courtly did when he died. I'm sure it's what killed him."

"We're going to need you to make a full statement on the record inside," Gene said to Bjorn.

Harry Liteman and the arresting officer now reached them as they pushed through the little crowd. Joshua Lantz stood there tense, with his arresting officer still gripping his upper arm firmly.

Gene addressed the guards. "Wait there a minute."

The arresting officers halted, expecting orders.

Gene turned to Bjorn. "We can ask for that chemical to be re-tested, if you know where it came from. The coroner doesn't have anything to test that substance against. So, if you can identify it...."

"Probably some bio-weapon, courtesy of Mayfounder," Bjorn sneered, "but I do know where it came from. I can show you the visual record I made."

Sarah leaned into Bjorn pointing to Harry Liteman, "Bjorn! That guy next to Joshua! It's the SP who searched my place!"

Bjorn replied quietly as he handed his recording device to Sammy, "Yeah, we got him. Alexandra found the helmet that helped identify him. Details later." He turned to Sammy, "All the proof is on there, Sammy. Harry's confession and proof of Mayfounder dumping."

Sammy Scribe quickly intercepted the device, hoping the SPs didn't see him slip it into his pocket.

Sarah turned toward Gene and asked, "Were Joshua's fingerprints or aura prints found on the inside of the violin?"

"On the outside case only," the officer clarified as he motioned to the two arresting officers to continue to stand-by. Harry's eyes darted anxiously from person to person. Joshua focused on his own feet.

"That Skipper Courtly," Sammy started, "always wanted to be the center of attention. It's almost like his craving the spotlight is what killed him. I wonder if the death certificate would state that pride is the official cause of death."

"Pride?" Bjorn asked. "That's it! Who hasn't been in the spotlight?" Bjorn became animated as he glanced at Joshua. "Pip had to be framed for the murder. That's why the set-up had to be more elaborate than something like a cut and dried shooting. If Pip is in prison, he can't collect on any inheritance. It sounds like the Courtly money is being funneled off to one specific source."

Gene turned to the officers, "Put actor Harry Liteman in interview room 1. Earth Farmer Joshua Lantz in interview room 4. Intern Alexandra Courtly in interview room 7. Stay with them."

As Gene mentioned Alexandra's last name, Bjorn and Sarah looked sharply at each other.

"But," Sammy started, "Pip is getting out on bail. The office story-alert notified us. That's why I came down and brought Sarah with me."

Attorney Atsushi had just posted bail for Pip and was now exiting SP Quarters with him. Bjorn watched Joshua and Harry as Pip walked passed them.

Then it happened.

Wheels shrieking, the black vehicle came tearing around a corner, heading straight for the little group on the sidewalk in front of the SP station entrance.

In a flash, Bjorn realized they were all there. Bjorn, Sarah, Sammy, Alexandra, Joshua, Pip, Atsushi, Harry Liteman, the arresting officers, and Detective Gene. They were all in the path of a furious vehicle, ready to smash them between the Soldier Police station wall and the front fender which emitted huge blinding strobe lights immediately disorienting them.

They scattered, just as the vehicle smashed into the stolid cement wall.

The lightning reflexes of the Soldier Police paid off as they yanked their charges to safety. Hearing the explosive sounds of the crash, more SPs streamed out from the building, attack-ready.

Detective Gene scrambled to his feet and hurried to the smashed vehicle to remark, "No driver. It's another drone."

Bjorn knew time was running out and took off heading to his rental vehicle. "I'm not going to let him float out of here, Sammy, without leaving even a credit trail to trace!"

Sammy limping from his awkward fall, got up and called to Bjorn, "Where are you going?"

Bjorn shouted over his shoulder, "Sammy, remember you're calling in that favor."

Sammy halted. "Got it," he shouted back, as Bjorn scrambled into the rental and drove off.

Sarah quickly brushed pebbles off the palms of her hands as she hurried to Detective Gene, "Sir. We need to talk about the Courtlys."

9 CHAPTER Year 2036: A Glass of Bubbly (Continuous Ch 83)

Bjorn roared down the road in his rental. The vehicle ahead of him was weaving through other traffic, but Bjorn was determined not to lose him.

The multi-lane highway drifted into an empty single-lane country road.

Bjorn's rental squealed to a stop when he spotted the vehicle he had followed was now parked and partially hidden in shrubbery. He slipped out of his rental.

Several yards away was a large grey warehouse. He pushed aside branches to get a better look. Nobody was around.

He first approached the parked vehicle, looked inside, and saw it was abandoned. Then, Bjorn walked toward the large building.

Were they inside? Bjorn was just moments behind them. How could they have moved so quickly? Had they changed vehicles and left this place already?

Then, he felt a sharp pain on the back of his head as white spots appeared and blackness followed. Bjorn sunk to the ground.

"What was that?" Pip asked.

"Somebody fell. Help me bring him inside," the other one replied.

They both went out and found a crumpled Bjorn Esterday on the ground. He was out cold.

"That's the reporter!" Pip exclaimed.

"Probably spying on you for a story. Let's bring him in."

They both struggled under the weight

of Bjorn's muscular frame. Pip's companion searched around for the best place to stash Bjorn. After removing Bjorn's com and vehicle-starter, Bjorn's limp body was placed into a loading cage, which already held empty receptacles and other construction refuse.

He turned the key on the gate of the cage.

"You're locking him in?" Pip asked.

"Just to give you enough time to get out of here. You know what pests paparazzi can be," Pip's companion smiled as he pushed the large red wall button that triggered the crane to lift the cage up and move it so that it was suspended over a dump truck.

"What are you doing to that reporter?" Pip asked.

"Every afternoon, the contents of the cage empties and the dump truck transports it to the recycle dissolution vats. That reporter will be out of the cage long before then."

"I've never heard of recycling something that totally dissolves. I'm not technical about that stuff." Pip slumped down onto an old crate. "This is not my idea of a fun celebration for getting out of jail," he whined.

"Here, sign this!" A crisp electronic tablet and stylus was presented to Pip. He obediently scanned his thumbprint and signed with the stylus.

"What is that," Pip asked. "Some agreement that says I don't have to show up in court and can call in, instead?"

"You, Pip, stand to inherit everything from Skipper Courtly. The paperwork declaring bankruptcy is filed, so you won't have to pay off any vendors... and all the money goes to you."

"Finally!" Pip smiled.

"And to celebrate, I brought champagne,"announced Pip's companion as he pulled out a dark green bottle with a gold label from an ice chest he had dragged in from the trunk of his car. He popped the cork and poured a frosty glass of champagne as he simpered, "Pip, you never actually wanted to run a bunch of companies, did you?"

He handed Pip the glass of champagne.

"No. You said I could just live off the dividends or something. Throw some parties for my friends. Spend it like I want to," said Pip accepting the glass of bubbly.

"And I have always supported you, haven't I?"

"Of course," Pip grinned, "That's why I'm gonna give you something like twenty percent of it all."

Pip slurped a long sip of champagne.

"I was thinking more like one hundred percent," came the smile, as Pip's face adopted a knitted brow.

Pip asked, "Let me see that thing I just signed. What was it?"

"It was a confession that you killed Skipper Courtly and out of remorse turned over all the remaining funds in all

Courtly business accounts... to... me, care of the Mayfounder Foundation. Before you commit suicide..."

"But," Pip was now fighting for words, "I never touched Dad. Wait... It was you, wasn't it?"

And with that, Pip collapsed.

10 CHAPTER Year 2036: Caged (Continuous Ch 84)

Bjorn stirred.

For some reason, his sluggish limbs felt heavy as if magnetized to the floor. His eyes refused to open. He lay there, feeling dizzy.

When he was finally able to open his eyes, he looked up and saw sky.

What was sky doing there?

He turned his head. It ached. The back of his head throbbed as it stung when he rolled his head against the floor to peer out the side of the cage.

Cage?

His eyes couldn't focus as sun shone through the cross hatched steel wires forming the walls of his prison.

Where was he? He couldn't remember getting here.

He turned his head in the other direction. The light was blocked with piles of empty canisters. Large oxygen tanks, smaller cans, all seemed empty.

Was he in a disposal unit?

Slowly he sat up, but the floor began to reel back and forth. He slapped both hands down, trying to gain his balance. Cautiously, he looked out and saw that nobody was around. After a moment, the swinging stopped.

Then, he realized he was suspended in air and really was in some sort of a cage. He looked out and down. He was very high up, suspended right over a dump truck, which appeared to be driverless.

Cautiously, he stood to his feet, keeping his knees slightly bent as one would in a rocking ship on the choppy ocean. Now looking around, he saw the door. He shook it, but it was padlocked.

He felt for his com device. Where was it? He searched the floor. Nope. It must have been removed. Was anything else missing?

Yes. His vehicle-starter. Gone. Even if he could get out of this cage, he wouldn't be able to drive away. Obviously, somebody thought he would soon be disposed of permanently, but just in case, they removed any means of escape for Bjorn.

He turned around and grabbed a large oxygen tank and checked that it was empty. Then, he swung at the lock. Then the hinges.

Nothing happened.

The loud noise of metal against metal reverberated and echoed in the distance. If anybody were around, they would have responded to the loud sound, but as the echoes faded, nothing.

He checked the smaller cans and, after some rummaging, he found one that didn't seem quite empty. He read the label. It might work.

He knew that steel becomes ridged when cooled even if it doesn't lose any tensile strength. He hoped that this can of difluoroethane would cool the lock sufficiently, about thirteen degrees below zero ought to do it. He hoped it wasn't one of those extra secure locks that would require metal to cool to forty below zero.

He sprayed the lock, waited a moment, then grabbed the empty oxygen tank again, and swung with all his might. The cage swayed, but the lock burst opened this time, flinging the door out wide.

Bjorn, still suspended high up at the ceiling, wrapped his fingers into the diamond-shaped lattice-work steel walls and climbed gingerly outside the cage. The cage swung with each movement he made. He pulled himself up to the cage roof. Then he grabbed the cable which attached the suspended cage to the crane's mechanical jib. Next, Bjorn crawled up the jib, to where it began sharply pointing down at a 45 degree angle.

He swung his legs around the jib of the crane and inched his way to the flat-sided perpendicular boom. Once he got onto the boom, he carefully slid down a hundred feet on his belly, feet first, until he finally landed on the roof of the operator cab.

From there, it was a simple jump from the top of the cab to the hood, then down to the ground.

He took a deep breath as he wiped his raw sweaty hands on his thighs.

Then, he heard a groan.

Across the floor, he saw a man sitting, his back propped against the wall, his face in shadow.

Bjorn didn't know if he should approach. Was this the man who had put him in the cage? Bjorn ducked out of sight and observed.

The man didn't move. Maybe he was asleep. Bjorn quickly evaluated if this was somebody who could help him, or someone who would attack.

Bjorn carefully approached, but tensed his muscles in case a rapid reaction to defend himself was needed.

Silently, he edged right up to the man. The man still didn't move. Bjorn shook him by the shoulder, but the man slid to one side, and without any noticeable reflexes, melted to the floor.

Then Bjorn saw his face.

Bjorn whispered, "Pip Courtly?"

Pip didn't respond. His champagne glass was nearly drained and still in his hand.

Bjorn grabbed Pip's wrist. Nothing. Then, Bjorn tried to find a pulse in Pip's neck. It was slow and thready.

Was Pip dying?

Bjorn looked around the huge space. Piles of crates and boxes obscured his view. He listened. No sounds from anywhere. The place was completely deserted. Confident he was alone, Bjorn searched around for something that might be useful.

In one corner, barely visible in the shadows, stood a dark blue battered truck. It was an old electric job. He ran to the truck and saw that it was plugged into the wall, being charged up.

He opened the cab door, pulled himself up behind the wheel, and pushed the key-less starter button. It whined to life.

He quickly got out, unplugged it from the wall, before whoever was charging it came back.

He gave the electric cord another tug and waited as it rewound itself up inside the body of the truck. He climbed back into the driver's seat.

As the truck hummed quietly, he maneuvered it through the narrow fully stocked aisles and drove to Pip.

Carefully, he picked Pip up and placed him in the back seat. With the tail of his shirt, he ran to retrieve the champagne glass that had lain next to Pip and placed it, without touching it, into the truck cup holder. Quickly buckling Pip securely, Bjorn raced to the driver's side and immediately strapped himself in.

The gauge read half charged. Maybe it was not enough of a charge to get to the hospital, but he'd have to chance it.

He drove toward the exit, and braked at the huge closed doors. He jumped out. The doors were not locked. He pushed hard and got the space wide enough to permit the tiny dark blue truck through the opening.

This wasn't the smoothest ride Bjorn ever had, he thought, as he bounced over speed bumps on the way out of the complex.

Pip groaned with each bump.

Good. He was still alive.

When Bjorn got onto the country road,

he headed back to town toward the hospital.

Pip muttered in his delirious state, "Dad chased ghosts. I dealt with the devil and lost. You'll catch him, right? I never hurt Dad. He did."

Then Pip fell silent and passed out.

"I'll find him if I can, Pip," Bjorn said to his unconscious passenger.

Bjorn honked the horn as he approached the hospital's emergency bay and got the attention of a paramedic.

"You can reach me at the Daily Memo," Bjorn started as he dragged Pip out of the back and carefully placed him on the ground by the door. "I think he's been poisoned or given an allergen. He seems to be dying. I found this..."

Bjorn shoved the half-empty champagne glass into the health worker's nitrile gloved hands and with what little charge remained in the truck, he drove off again, leaving Pip at the feet of this very confused medical worker.

16 CHAPTER- What will happen next?

We see that Bjorn actually gets proof of the original Earth Farmer complaint that toxic waste is being dumped onto farm land. Will Bjorn get this proof safely to the right people?

Is the poison Bjorn discovers the same poison that killed Skipper Courtly?

Is the dump truck that regularly carries poison waste to the farmland actually from the foundation that Skipper Courtly himself created, years earlier?

72

Is the driverless vehicle that shows up behind Bjorn on his way back to town, just following Bjorn's rental vehicle, or is it following Bjorn himself? Who would be following Bjorn?

What must Bjorn do now that he has learned the identity of the fake SP who ransacked Sarah's place?

Why was Pip being released from the SP Station when he is clearly a person of interest?

Earlier, why was Joshua Lantz brought into the SP station for questioning about the Skipper Courtly murder?

With all the possible suspects gathered together in front of the SP station, who ordered the driverless vehicle to ram into that crowd? Who was the intended target?

Now, in today's reading, Pip is presented with his freedom after he's been tricked into giving away all his Courtly fortune. Can he do anything to protect himself before the poisoned champagne takes effect?

Who will be the new monarch of the Courtly kingdom?

Was Pip betrayed or is this all part of the plan?

Can Sammy Scribe be trusted?

After Bjorn drops off PIP at the hospital, where does he race away to?

&o To Be Continued... cs

17 Did You Know

By 2005, independent studies demonstrated that active recycling contributes millions of dollars to each state's economy.

The recycling and reuse industry consists of approximately 56,000 establishments that employ over 1.1 million people. In addition, they generate an annual payroll of nearly $37 billion, and gross over $236 billion in annual revenues. The recycling and reuse industry generates billions in federal, state, and local tax revenues (estimated at $12.9 billion in 2001).

About 4 percent of total energy consumption in the U.S. is used in the production of all plastic products. For example, recycling one single ton of paper saves the equivalent of 17 trees and 7,000 gallons of water.

Pennsylvania, back in 2009, released the impact of recycling at that point in time: Recycling and Reuse Establishments: 3,800; Recycling and Reuse Employment: 52,316 jobs; Annual Sales Receipts: $20.6 billion; Annual Payroll: $2.2 billion

South Carolina also did a study which showed about 45,000 recycling jobs are expected beyond the year 2000, over 20,000 of which should come from the manufacturing sector.

In addition, Massachusetts found total value to be added by manufacturing sectors (recycling): $588,029,000

The EPA (Environmental Protection Agency) reports that more than 36 million TONS of food is wasted each year, dumped into land fills, and left to break down into methane and other noxious gasses. This also adds to air pollution. So, the EPA suggest some ideas to avoid wasting food:

✓ Shop in your refrigerator first. Make sure your fridge is empty before you go shopping again. Use up what you have.

✓ Buy only what you really will use.

✓ Buy in bulk to save money only if you will use all the food before it spoils.

✓ Donate untouched food, that you no longer want, to food banks to help the hungry in your area.

✓ In seasons with a lot of food sold in the stores, freeze, preserve, or can extra fruits and vegetables.

✓ At restaurants, take home left overs and use them for your next meal.

✓ Put food into compost piles instead of throwing it away.

ABOUT Wynter Sommers

Wynter Sommers is the pseudonym for an American writing team, which harnesses multiple skills in technology, research, and education. Formally trained with a PhD in Education, Wynter Sommers blends academic classroom experience, with corporate sophistication, and a passion for developing more effective student insights.

Wynter Sommers has taught classrooms of enthusiastic children. She has a heart to inspire creativity and develop critical thinking skills, all to encourage students to make wise choices in life. She wants to impart the talent of honing one's skills in self-reliance and collaborative team work. Despite any environmental barriers outside of an individual's control, Wynter Sommers wishes to impart the message that genuine hope, love, and peace can help us overcome obstacles, and cement friendships. Wynter Sommers hopes you enjoy the other *Bjorn Esterday Was not Born Yesterday* stories in this series.

www.ingramcontent.com/pod-product-compliance
Lightning Source LLC
Chambersburg PA
CBHW051842020726
47502CB00005B/1917